The Ancient
Liangzhu
Unlocking its Secrets

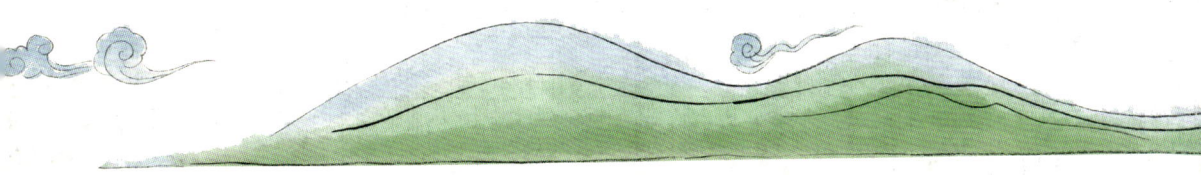

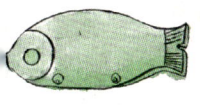

First published in the UK in 2021
by Little Steps Publishing
Uncommon, 126 New King's Rd, London SW6 4LZ
www.littlestepspublishing.co.uk
ISBN: 978-1-912678-30-3
Text copyright © 2021 Liu Bin and Yu JingJing • Illustrations copyright © 2021 Zeng Qiqi

All rights reserved.

The rights of Liu Bin and Yu JingJing to be identified as the author and Zeng Qiqi to be identified as the illustrator of this work have been asserted.

This book is sold subject to the condition that it shall not, by way of trade or otherwise, be lent, hired out or otherwise circulated in any form of binding or cover other than that in which it is published. No part of this publication may be reproduced, stored in a retrieval system, or transmitted in any form or by any means (electronic, mechanical, photocopying, recording or otherwise) without the prior written permission of Little Steps Publishing.

A CIP catalogue record for this book is available from the British Library.
Translated by Qin Ling • Designed by Verity Clark • Printed in China
10 9 8 7 6 5 4 3 2 1

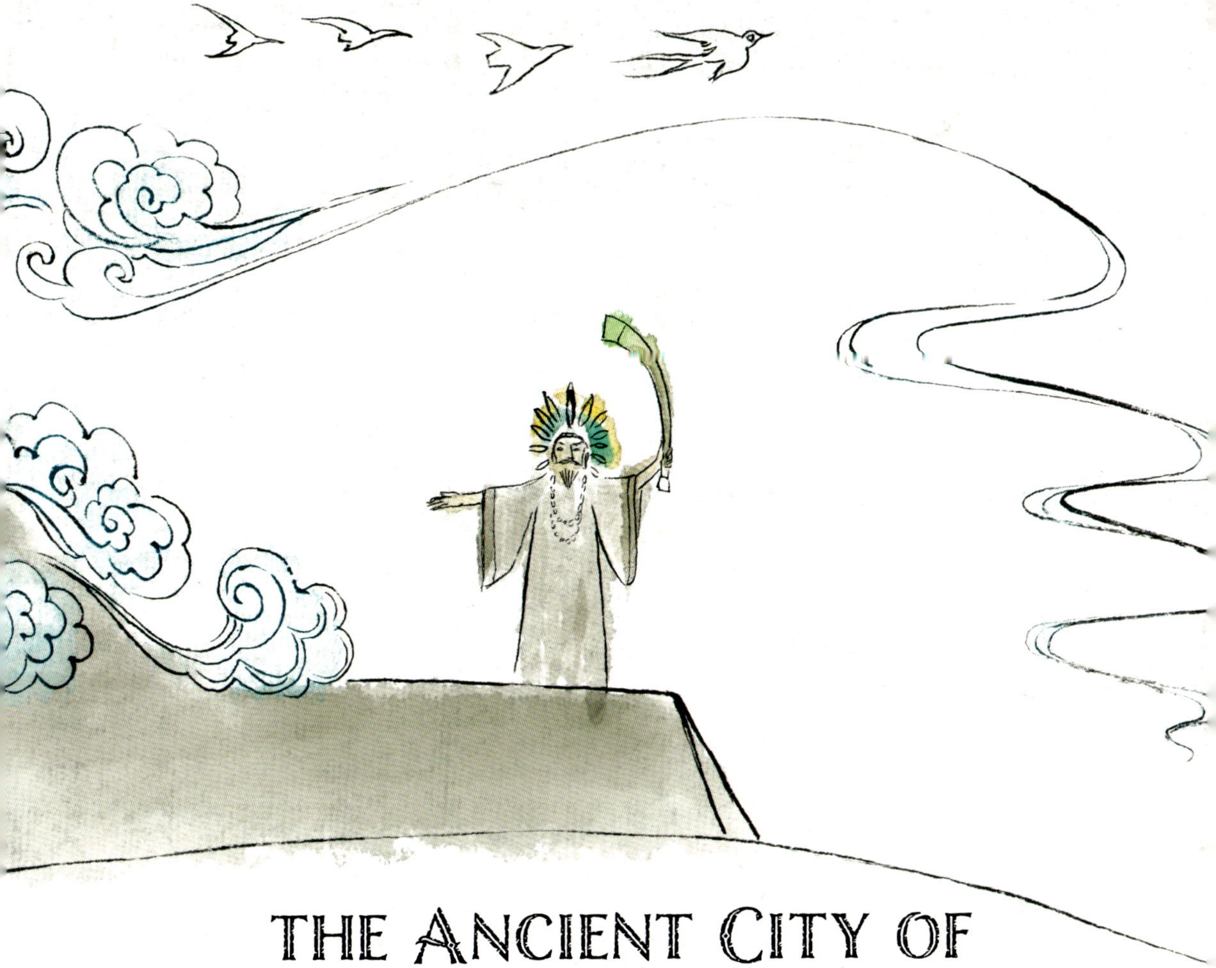

THE ANCIENT CITY OF LIANGZHU

UNLOCKING ITS SECRETS

WRITTEN BY
LIU BIN & YU JINGJING

ILLUSTRATED BY
ZENG QIQI

Little Steps

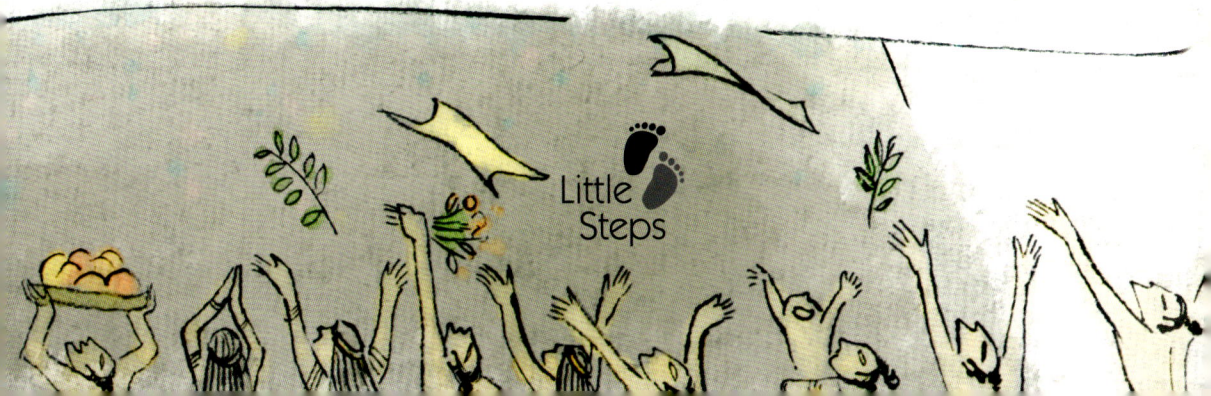

CONTENTS

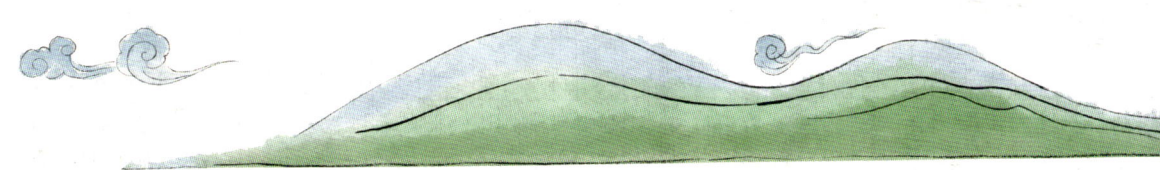

6   WATER
A MYSTERIOUS ANCIENT CIVILISATION EMERGES AMONG RIVERS AND LAKES

38 CITY
BORDERED BY MOUNTAINS, IN THE MIDDLE OF A PLAIN, A MAGNIFICENT ANCIENT CITY RISES UP

70 JADE
SKILLED CRAFTSMEN CARVE SYMBOLS INTO JADE, OFFERING CLUES ABOUT THEIR ANCIENT GODS AND BELIEFS

WATER

The Liangzhu people, who lived 5000 years ago, were lucky. They lived in the beautiful Taihu Basin, where the river waters were clear, the trees were green and lush, and the white cranes flew overhead.

The Liangzhu people, who lived 5000 years ago, were hardworking. Living along waterways, they fished and grew rice, fed pigs and silkworms, built homes and made pottery.

The Liangzhu people, who lived 5000 years ago, were wise. Faced with the challenges of storms and floods, they built the earliest dam systems in the world to control the flow of water.

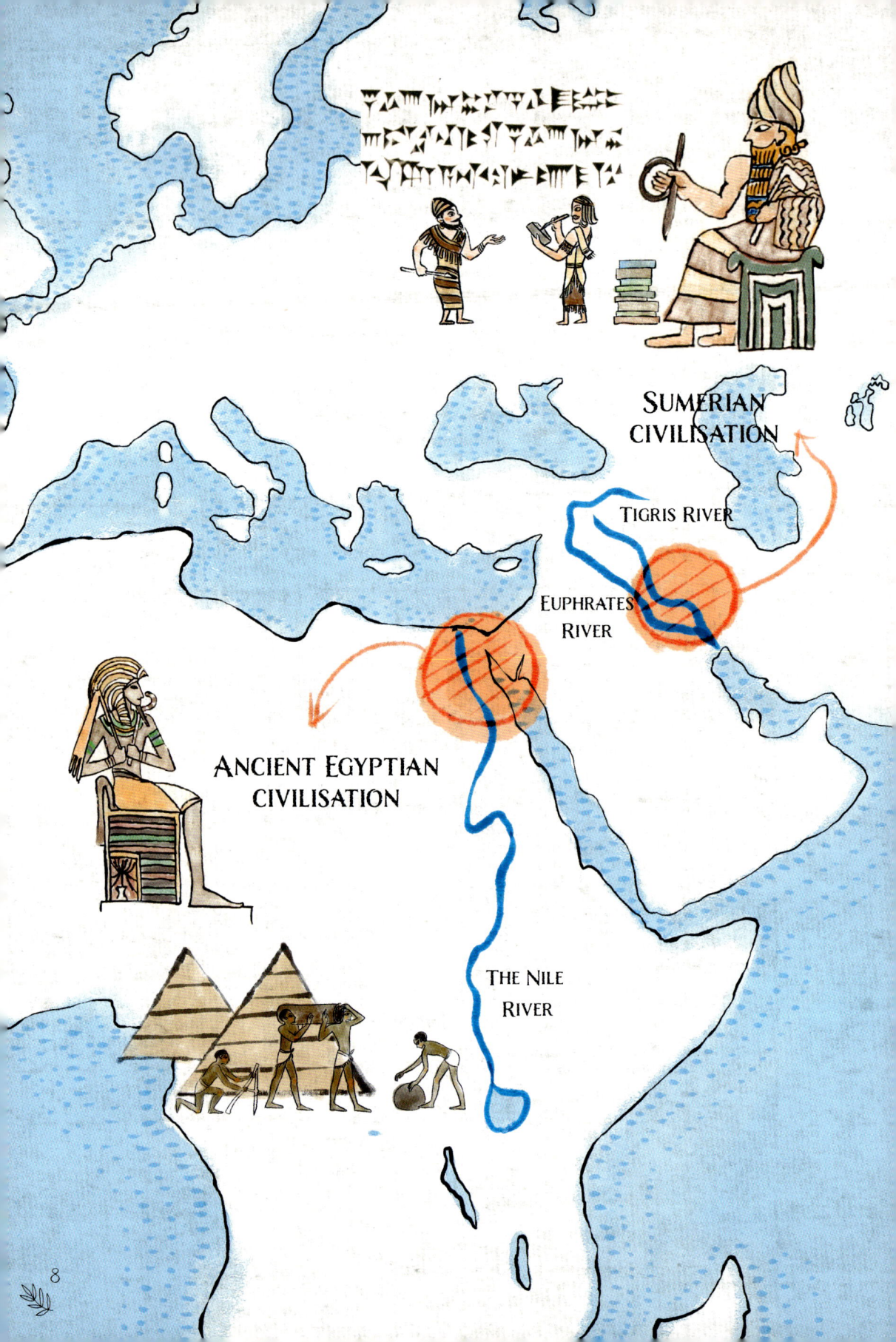

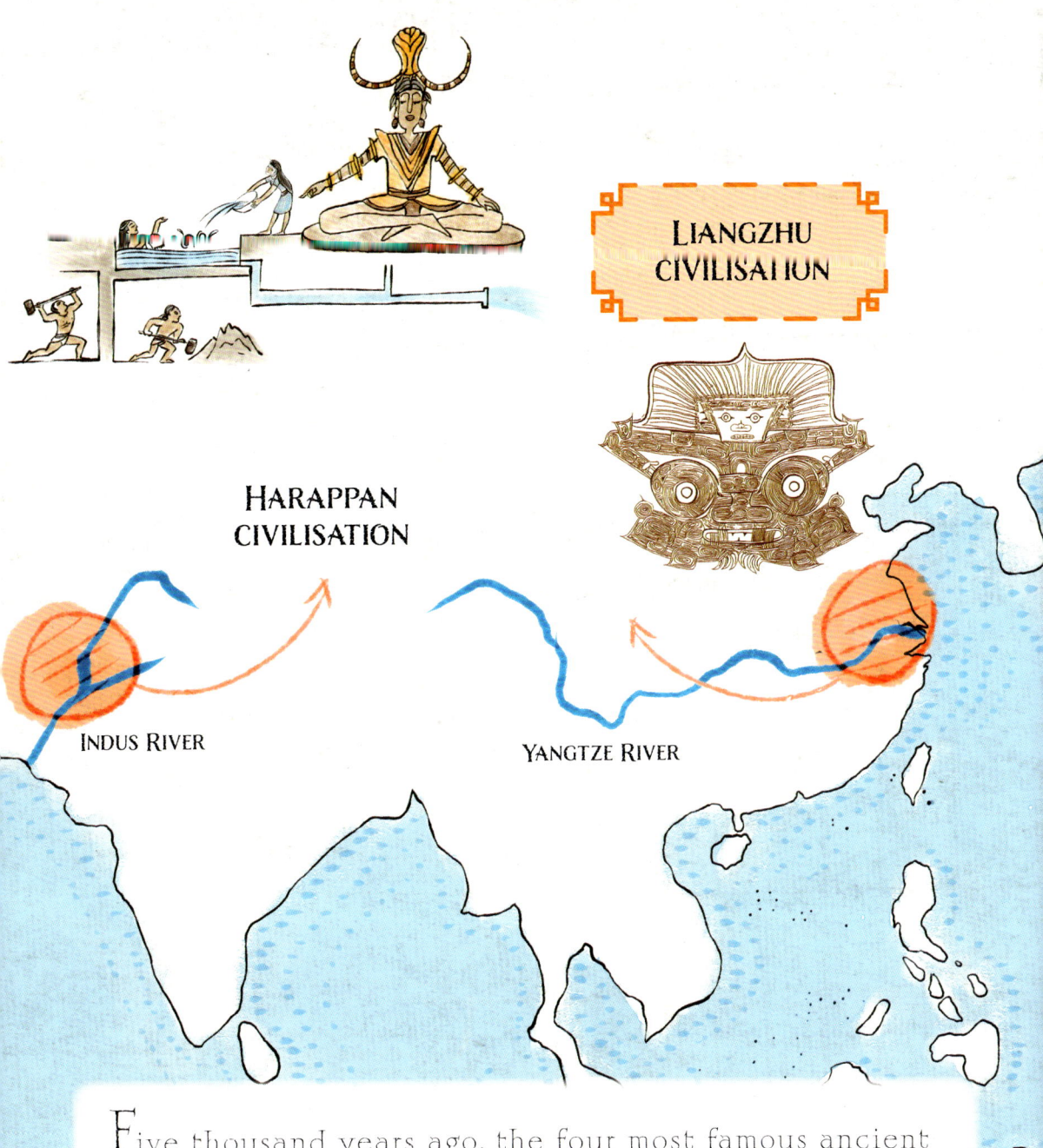

Five thousand years ago, the four most famous ancient civilisations all grew along rivers.

The Yangtze, the longest river in Asia and the third-longest river in the world, has a beautiful and vast river plain that reaches towards the sea.

Here, the Liangzhu civilisation emerged.

The Taihu Basin, on the Yangtze river plain, is densely covered with waterways, and the climate is warm and humid. This is where the Liangzhu people lived.

Five thousand years ago, in most parts of the world, people ate wheat, barley and different types of millet. The Liangzhu people were different. They grew and cultivated crops of rice.

Rice

Rice is one of the oldest crops in the world, and one of the most important to human civilisations. But where did rice come from?

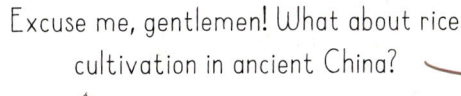

Here is the history of rice in Zhejiang, Eastern China, as told by archaeologists.

Archaeologists are still working hard to find out where rice cultivation began...

10,000 YEARS AGO: Shangshan people, from the Pujiang River, ate rice.

7000–8000 YEARS AGO: Kuahuqiao and Hemudu people in Zhejiang province, eastern China, began to cultivate rice plants.

5000 YEARS AGO: Liangzhu people planted rice in large paddy fields.

11

Around 10,000 years ago, ancient peoples began to manage and cultivate rice. The Lower Yangtze was one area of early rice cultivation.

The Liangzhu people used ploughs to make the ground ready for the rice plants. Ploughing the soil is much quicker and more efficient than using a shovel or a hoe.

The Songze people, who lived in the Taihu Basin just before the Liangzhu period, began to use stone sickles to cut and harvest their rice plants. The Liangzhu people also used them.

One side of the sickle blade is slanted, so right-handed and left-handed people use different sickles. Interestingly, 90 per cent of all Liangzhu sickles that have been found were designed for left-handed people. Does that mean Liangzhu people were mostly left-handed?

After harvesting their rice plants, the Liangzhu people hung them up to dry, then transported them to a granary for storage.

Archaeologists have found large granaries in the ancient city of Liangzhu. These were able to store hundreds of thousands of kilograms of rice.

Fishing

Water not only nourished rice plants for the Liangzhu people. It also provided a home for many aquatic creatures.

The Liangzhu people's diet included several species of carp, snakehead fish, turtles, tortoises, crabs, clams and snails.

Boats for fishing were essential to the Liangzhu people.

At the Kuahuqiao site, where people lived 8000 years ago, archaeologists found a huge canoe and two wooden paddles. The canoe was carved from one giant piece of pine wood.

In 2010, archaeologists found another wooden canoe that was more than 7 metres long. This came from Maoshan, a site from the Liangzhu period.

Many wooden paddles have been excavated from Liangzhu sites. Compared to older paddles from the earlier Hemudu culture, Liangzhu's are longer and wider, making them better for paddling.

The Liangzhu people had many ways to catch fish. They used nets and spears, and made fish traps by weaving bamboo. Fish could swim into the traps but could not swim out again.

Gathering

The Liangzhu people loved fruits and vegetables.
 They ate peaches, apricots, plums, persimmons, water chestnuts and bottle gourds.

19

Hunting

Besides cultivating rice, fishing and gathering, the Liangzhu people also hunted animals for meat using bows and arrows. Their arrows could be used as weapons too.

Deer and boar were the most common animals the Liangzhu people hunted. Wild boar were captured and tamed, eventually becoming domesticated pigs.

Pottery making

The Liangzhu people made different types of pottery for cooking and serving their food.

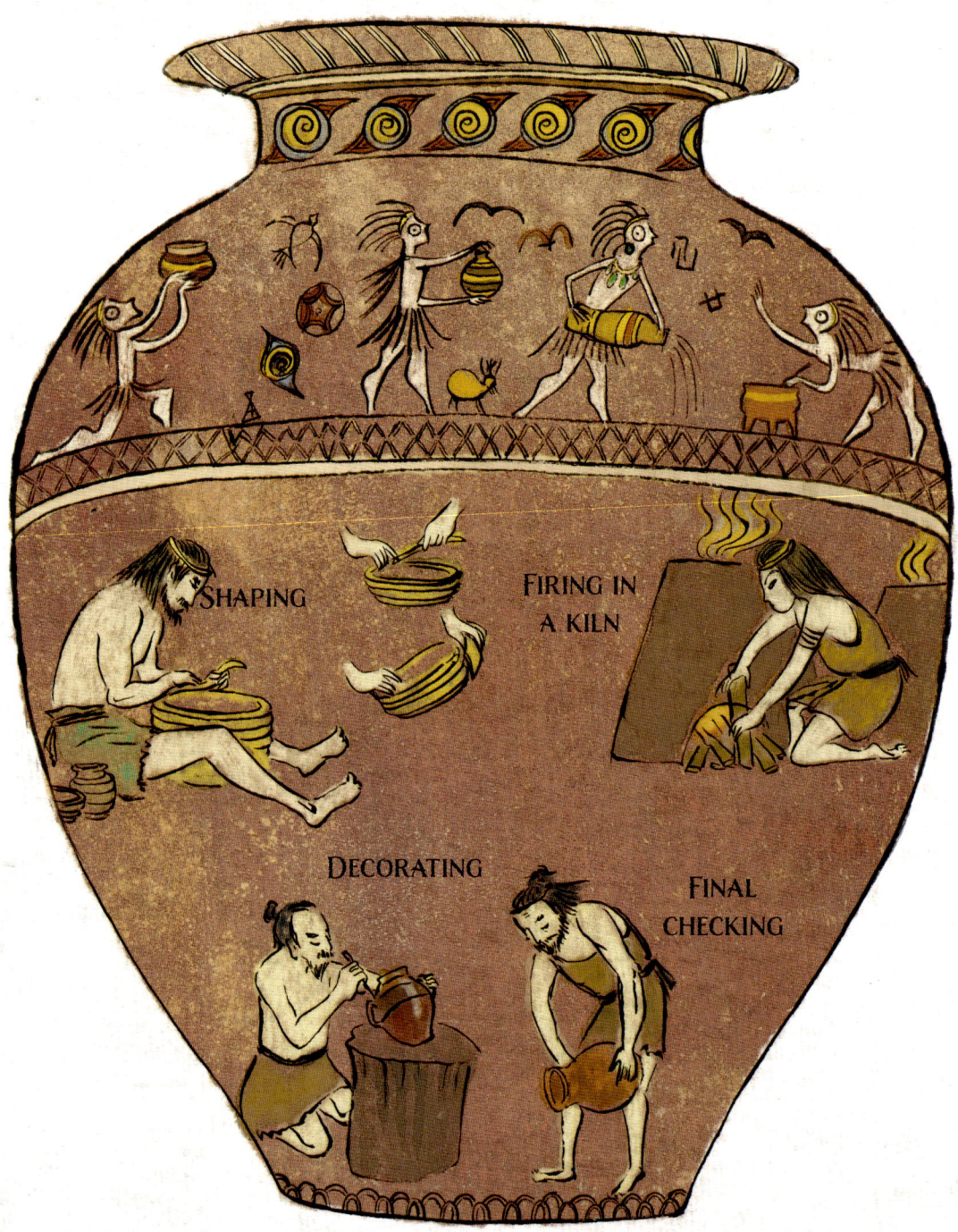

Shaping

Firing in a kiln

Decorating

Final checking

BOWL (*BO*)

THREE-LEGGED KETTLE/COOKER (*GUI*)

STEMMED PLATE (*DOU*)

Liangzhu people were real foodies. They made different types of pottery for cooking and serving their food.

THREE-LEGGED COOKER (*DING*)

POT (*GUAN*)

BASIN (*PEN*)

PLATE (*PAN*)

DRINKING VESSEL WITH 'EARS' AND A LID (*HU*)

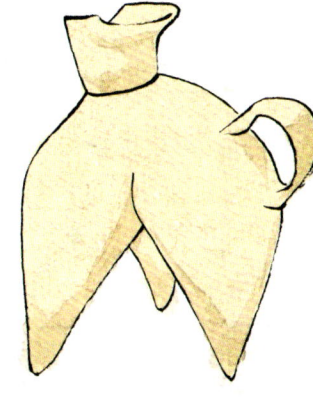

JAR (*GANG*)

THREE-LEGGED KETTLE/COOKER (*GUI*) WITH 'BAGGY' HOLLOW LEGS

25

Engraved symbols

The Liangzhu people also engraved various symbols on the pottery they made. Ancient peoples who did not yet have a writing system often made simple drawings like these. Their drawings later developed into writing systems - like the hieroglyphics of ancient Egypt, the cuneiform writings of Mesopotamia, the Chinese characters of ancient China and the hieroglyphics of the Mayan culture.

ENGRAVED SYMBOL → **ORACLE BONE SCRIPT** → **BRONZE INSCRIPTIONS**

REGULAR SCRIPT ← **CLERICAL SCRIPT** ← **SEAL SCRIPT**

PRINTING FONT

Chinese characters are the oldest writing system still in use today.

The symbols on these pottery pieces have not yet been deciphered. What do you think they mean?

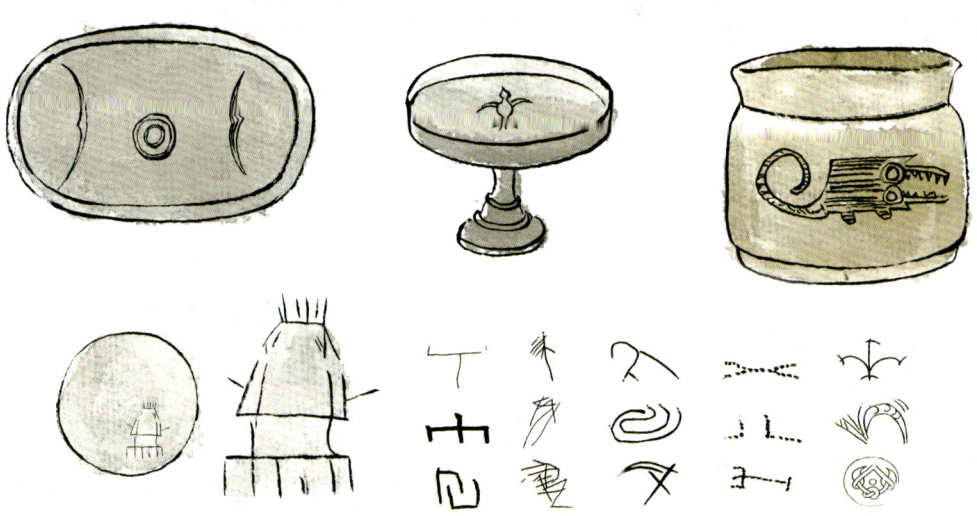

The symbols inscribed on Liangzhu pottery appeared individually but also in groups.

There is one pottery jar from the Liangzhu culture that has 12 consecutive symbols carved on it. Some palaeographers (experts who study ancient scripts) have suggested that these symbols represent the story of a tiger hunt.

Ever since this pottery jar was unearthed, people have been guessing what these symbols mean!

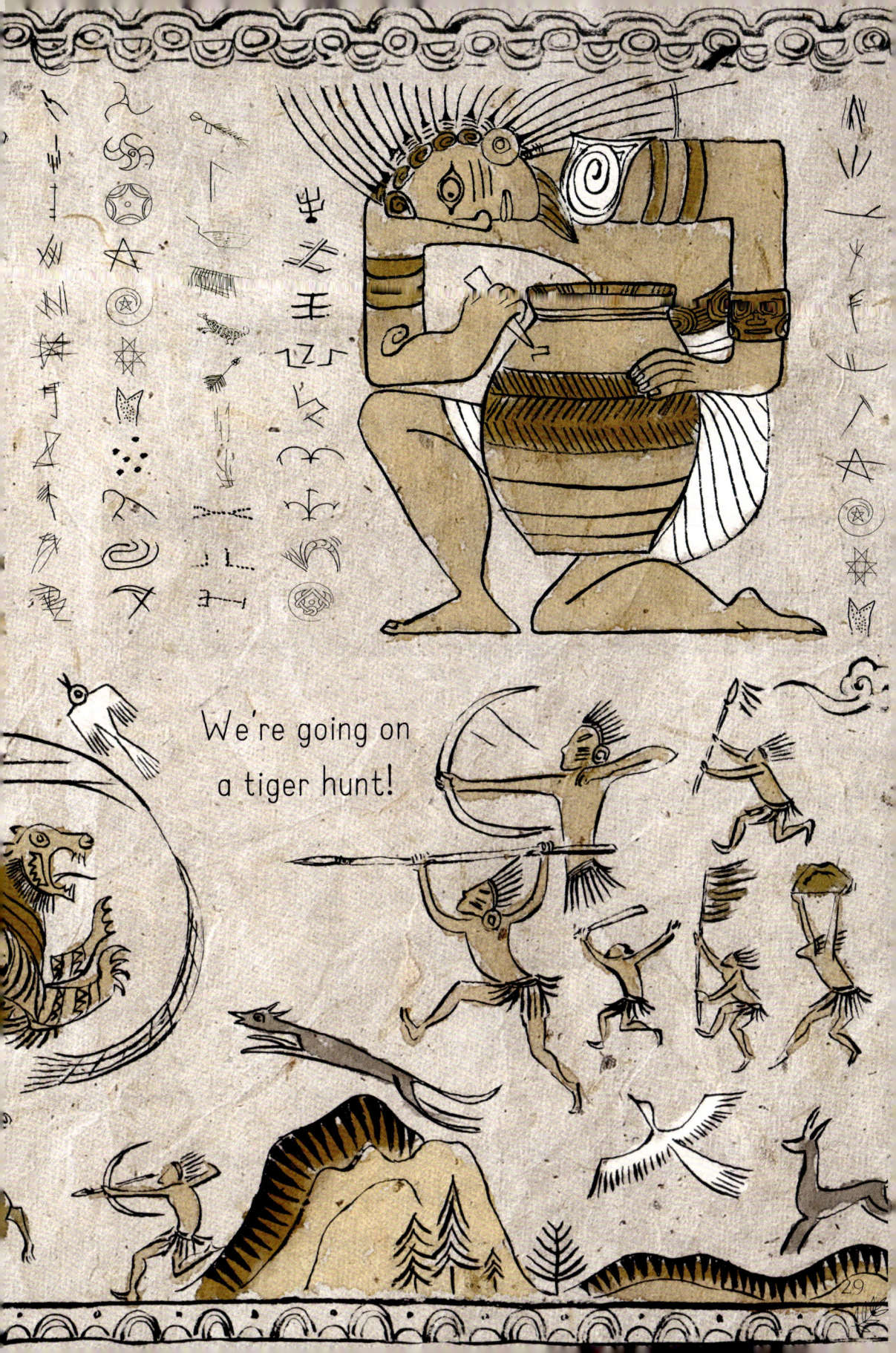

The looms and spindle whorls that the Liangzhu nobles used for spinning and weaving thread were sometimes made of jade, a very beautiful and valuable mineral.

SPINDLE W

Textiles

There are many mulberry trees in the Taihu Basin, and the Liangzhu people knew how to feed mulberry leaves to silkworms and make silk from the cocoons. However, the clothes people wore were mostly made from plant fibres, not silk.

Ramie is a plant from China that has a unique fibre. It is known as 'Chinese grass'.

The lives of the Liangzhu people were not always peaceful. They faced great challenges from storms and floods.

After the summer rainstorms, flash floods were disastrous for the villages in the Taihu Basin. But how could the Liangzhu people control the flow of water?

Controlling water

The clever Liangzhu people designed and built a huge water management system. To build dams, they invented the 'grass-wrapped silt' method, wrapping soil inside brick-sized bags made of reeds and the leaves of the cogongrass plant.

Don't underestimate these straw bags: they were an early form of the bricks we use today. Straw bags made it easier to produce and transport the building materials for the dams, and to reinforce the dam walls.

The Liangzhu straw-bag system allowed large groups of people to build dams, city walls and palaces in a short time. When archaeologists found the remains of the Liangzhu city walls, they were surprised when they opened a straw bag and found a blooming flower preserved inside!

The water technology of the Liangzhu people was very advanced. Their dam system was one of the earliest large-scale water systems in China, and one of the first dam systems in the world. The Liangzhu water system consisted of 11 dams that protected an area of about 100 square kilometres around the ancient city of Liangzhu.

EMBANKMENT

The Liangzhu people also dug artificial waterways inside and outside the central city, allowing for water transport in and out.

CITY

Around 5000 years ago, the Liangzhu people built their city on the wetland plain in what is now Yuhang, in Zhejiang province. They used the mountains as their boundary.

In the centre of the Liangzhu city was a terrace where palaces were built. The terrace was more than 10 metres high, with an area of about 280,000 square metres (almost 0.3 square kilometres). Around the terraces, the inner city covered about 3 square kilometres, making it four times as large as the famous Forbidden City palace complex in Beijing.

The outer city area was a little more than 6 square kilometres, with the water management system of dams and reservoirs on its north and west sides. The furthest dam from the city was more than 10 kilometres away.

The Liangzhu site is one of the largest city sites in China from the Neolithic period. When it was discovered in 2007 it was called 'The First City of China'. It is estimated that more than 10,000 people lived here 5000 years ago.

Choosing a site for the city

Before they decided where to build their city, the Liangzhu people carefully investigated the surrounding geography.

They chose a site that was in the centre of a plain bordered by mountains: Daxiong Mountain, Dazhe Mountain and, to the west, the Yao Mountain of ancient Pingyao Town. From the centre of the city to the foothills of each mountain was 3 kilometres.

LAKE TAIHU

From the nearby mountains, the people of the ancient Liangzhu city were able to obtain stone, wood and other supplies. The East Tiao River and the Liangzhu Port were close by, and the vast river network was very convenient for fishing and water transport. The plains were also perfect for growing rice.

WOOD

LIANGZHU CITY

STONE

Planning the city

Location, location, location! The city has to be between those mountains. We need to show we're in the centre of the world.

So, how should we begin building our city?

I suggest we intercept the upstream valley to prevent flooding and help transport wood from the upper area — and also set up fish farming.

Well, I think we should first build the observatories, and have sacrifice ceremonies on those altars at Yaoshan and Huiguanshan.

43

The Liangzhu people were forward-thinking. They knew that to build their city, they would have to control the flow of water.

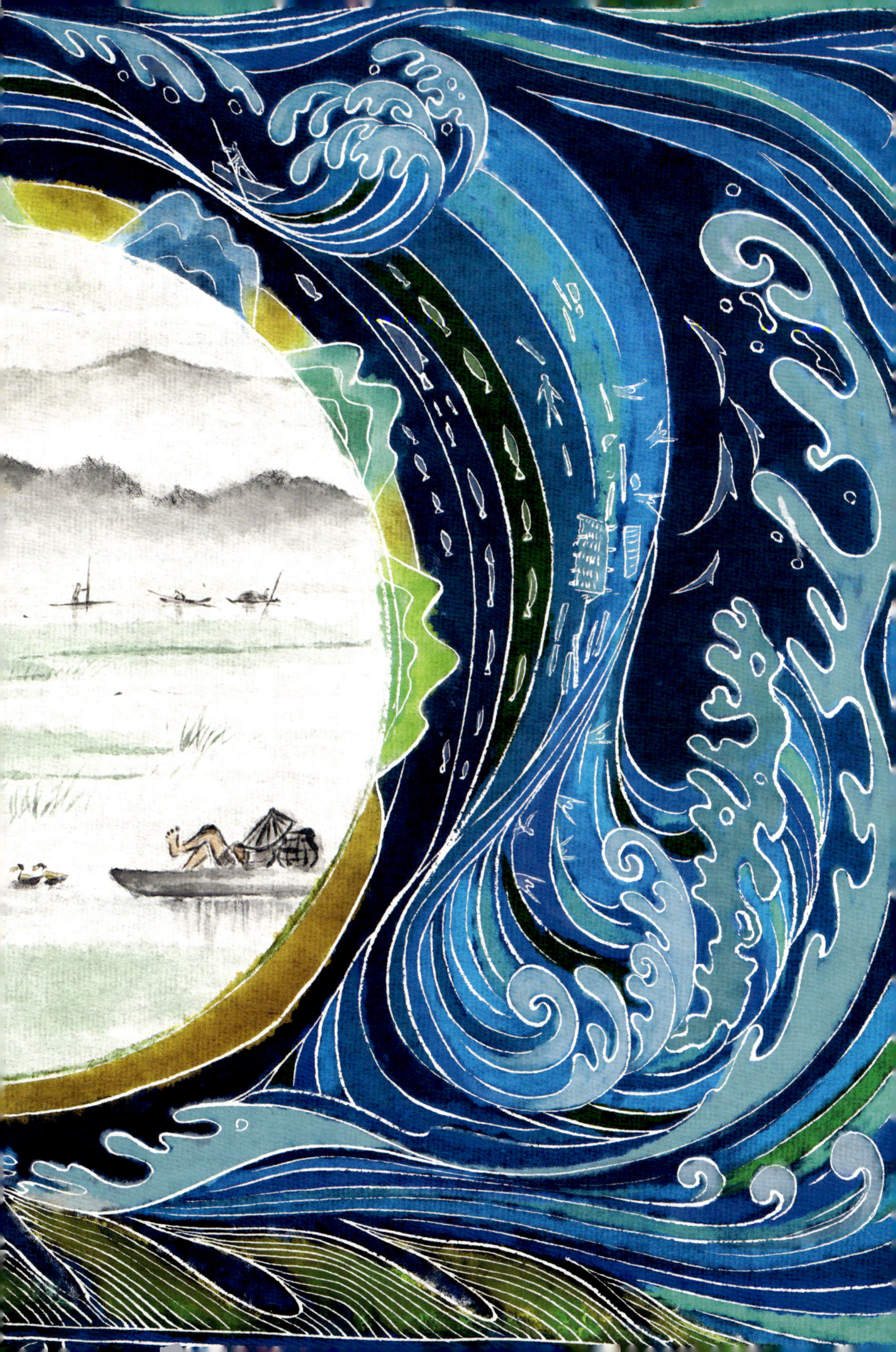

Palaces

The city's palaces were also very important. In the centre of the city, the Liangzhu people constructed a terrace 12-16 metres high, which served as the foundation for the palaces. Archaeologists call this area 'Mojiaoshan'.

The entire terrace is now 630 metres long from east to west and 450 metres wide from north to south. It was made from more than 2 million cubic metres of soil. Between the palaces, the people used sand and clay to build an open square of 70,000 square metres.

Archaeologists have found that there are no 'time gaps' between the layers that formed the platform. This shows that the terrace was built in a very short time.

What are those people doing?

0.6 METRES

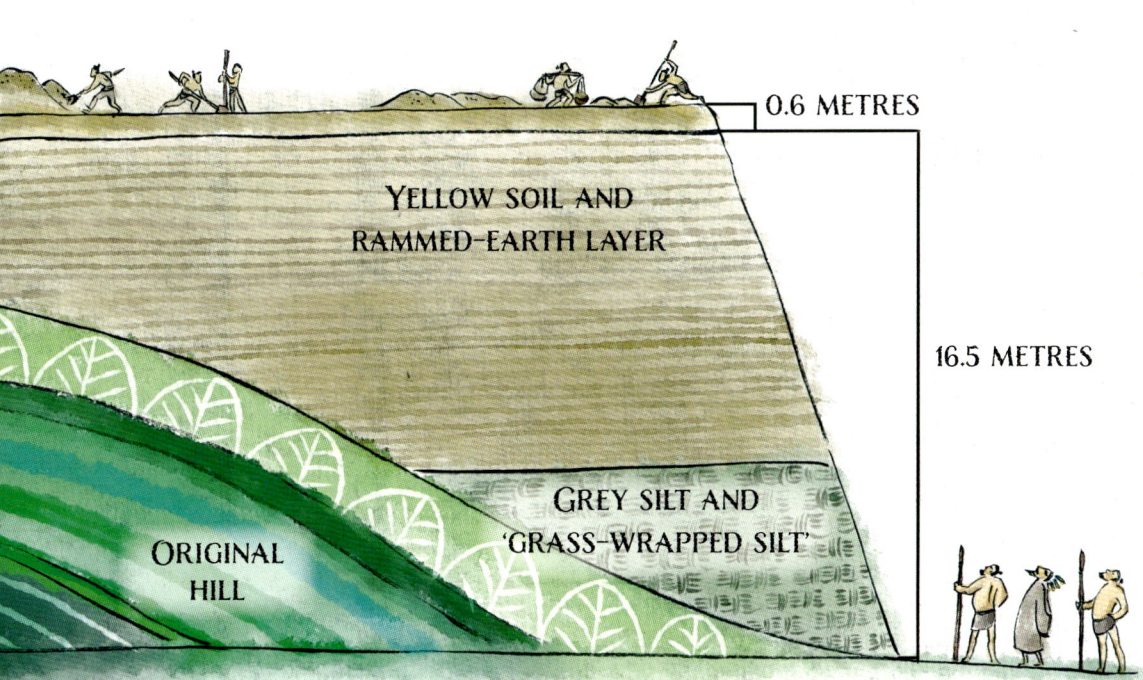

YELLOW SOIL AND
RAMMED-EARTH LAYER

16.5 METRES

ORIGINAL
HILL

GREY SILT AND
'GRASS-WRAPPED SILT'

The Liangzhu people cut and transported huge pieces of timber to build the palaces on top of Mojiaoshan.

Archaeological excavations have uncovered single pieces of wood that are 14–17 metres long.

Five thousand years ago, the Liangzhu king stood on this high platform and looked out over his city. He must have felt very proud!

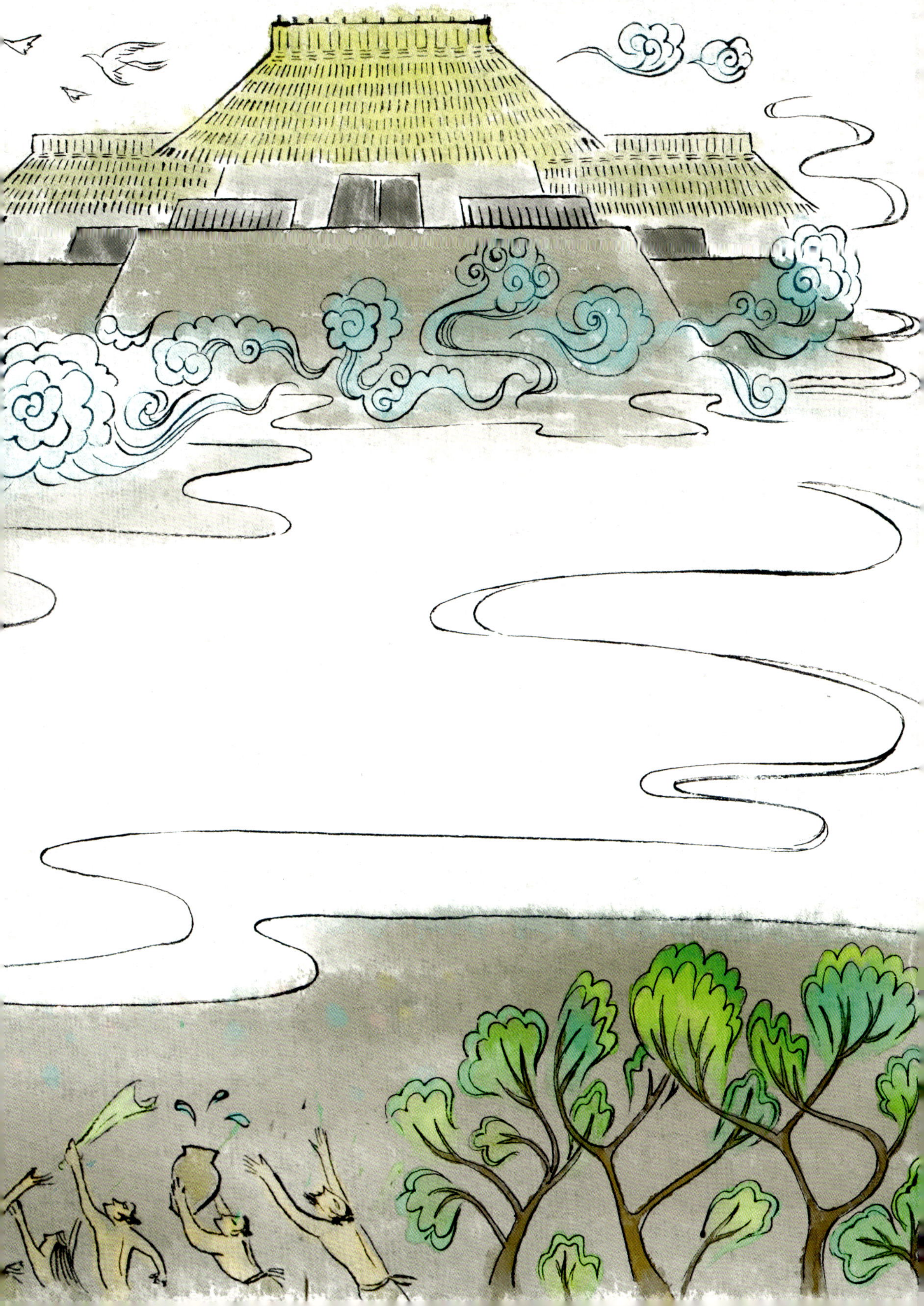

Altars

The Liangzhu people set up two ceremonial platforms to observe the sun, the moon and the stars. These are called altars. One was at Yaoshan, in the north-east of the city, and the other was at Huiguanshan in the north-west.

53

SUMMER SOLSTICE

AUTUMN EQUINOX

SPRING EQUINOX

WINTER SOLSTICE

T he Liangzhu altars are regarded as some of the earliest astronomical instruments in the world. People used them to observe the rising and setting sun. This was thousands of years before the first sundials were used in China to observe shadows and measure time.

SPRING EQUINOX

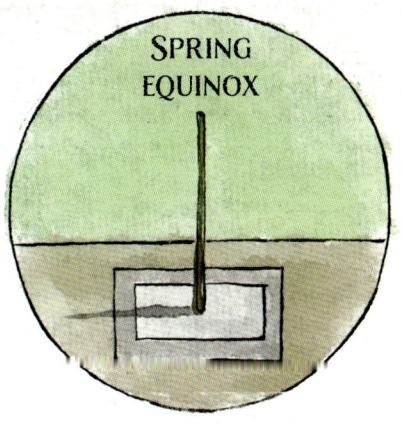

The sun rises from the east side of the frame on the altar and falls to the west.

SUMMER SOLSTICE

The sun rises from the north-east of the frame and falls north-west.

AUTUMN EQUINOX

The sun rises from the east side of the frame and falls to the west.

WINTER SOLSTICE

The sun rises from the south-east of the frame and falls south-west.

Generations of Liangzhu people observed the sunrise and sunset, watched the changes in the shadows, and recorded the trajectories of the sun and the moon in the sky. Gradually this information formed an astronomical calendar, which helped the Liangzhu people plan their crops and harvests.

The Yaoshan altar was also used for religious rituals and sacrifices. Some of the Liangzhu kings and nobles were buried here after their death.

Look – that's where I was buried!

Dazhe Mountain

Building the city

After building their dams and palaces, the Liangzhu people planned and built magnificent city walls.

DAXIONG MOUNTAIN

58

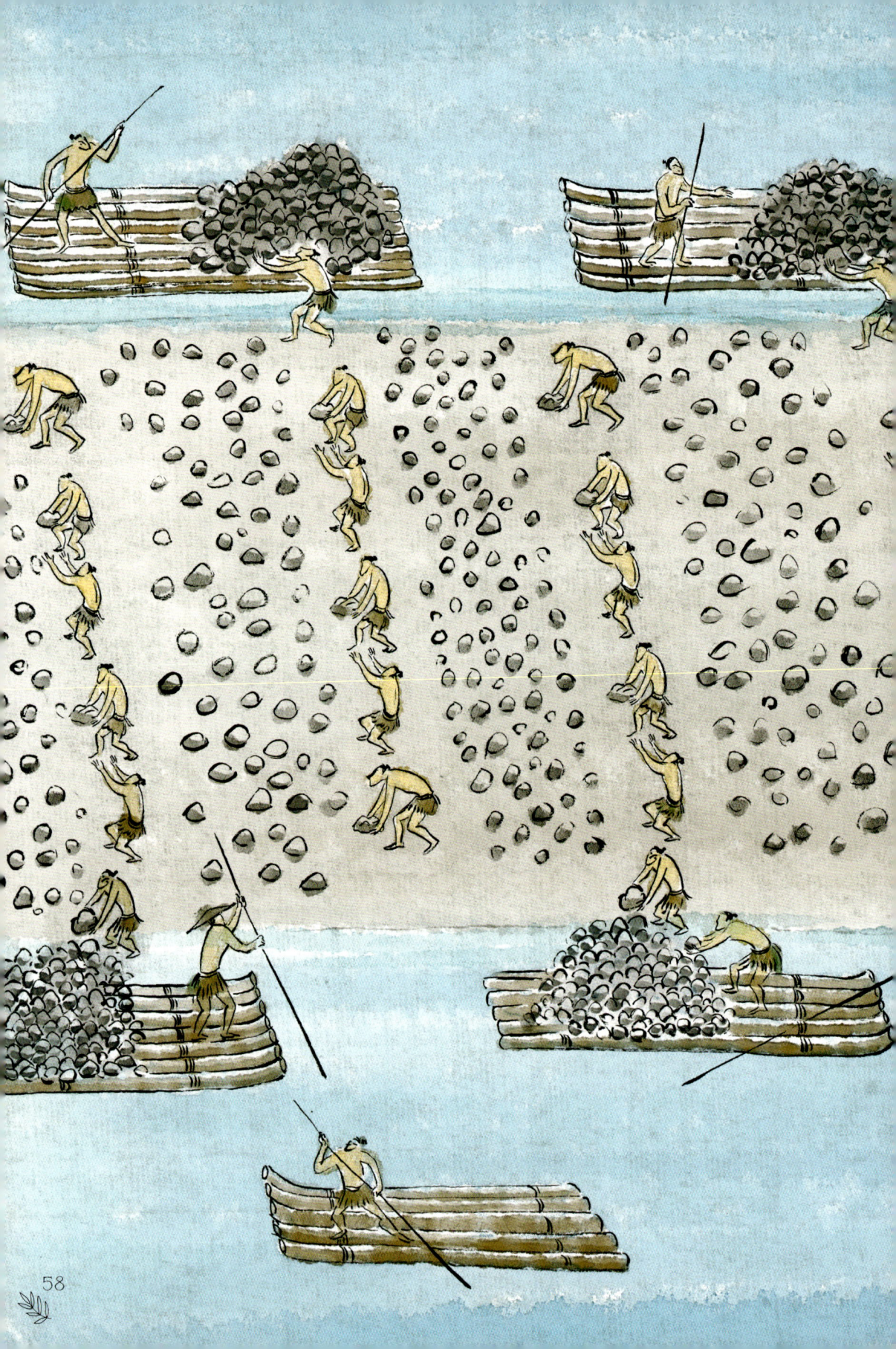

Usually, when building a city wall, people first dig a moat and then use the soil from the moat to build the wall. But the Liangzhu people laid stones as the foundation for their walls.

The ancient city of Liangzhu was built on wet, marshy ground. Its walls needed a strong stone foundation to guard against the water that rose from the wet ground, and to prevent floods.

Once the stone foundation was paved, the Liangzhu people used yellow soil from the nearby mountains to build the wall on top of it.

How grand was the scale of the ancient city of Liangzhu? Let's take a look at the city walls.

Each side of the wall had a length of more than 1500 metres. The wall was not only long but also thick: the narrowest part was about 20 metres, and the widest was about 150 metres.

Existing Wall: 4 metres

The highest part of the wall that still remains is part of the North Wall. It is 4 metres high. According to this, archaeologists have estimated how much labour would have been needed to build the city walls. Assuming that three people could dig one cubic metre of soil per day with stone tools, it would take 10,000 people a full year to build the city walls.

Remember that builders also need tools and food, as well as other support. It takes a lot of organisation to build dams and huge city walls – the Liangzhu people must have been very good at organising their society 5000 years ago!

**CITY GATE
(ON LAND)**

**CITY GATE
(ON WATER)**

The ancient city of Liangzhu was a city of water. A network of rivers crisscrossed the whole inner city. Outside the city were huge lakes, each hundreds of metres wide, in the east, north and west.

The Liangzhu people mainly relied on waterways for transport. There were nine gates in the Liangzhu city walls. Eight of these were water gates. The only land-based city gate was in the middle of the South Wall.

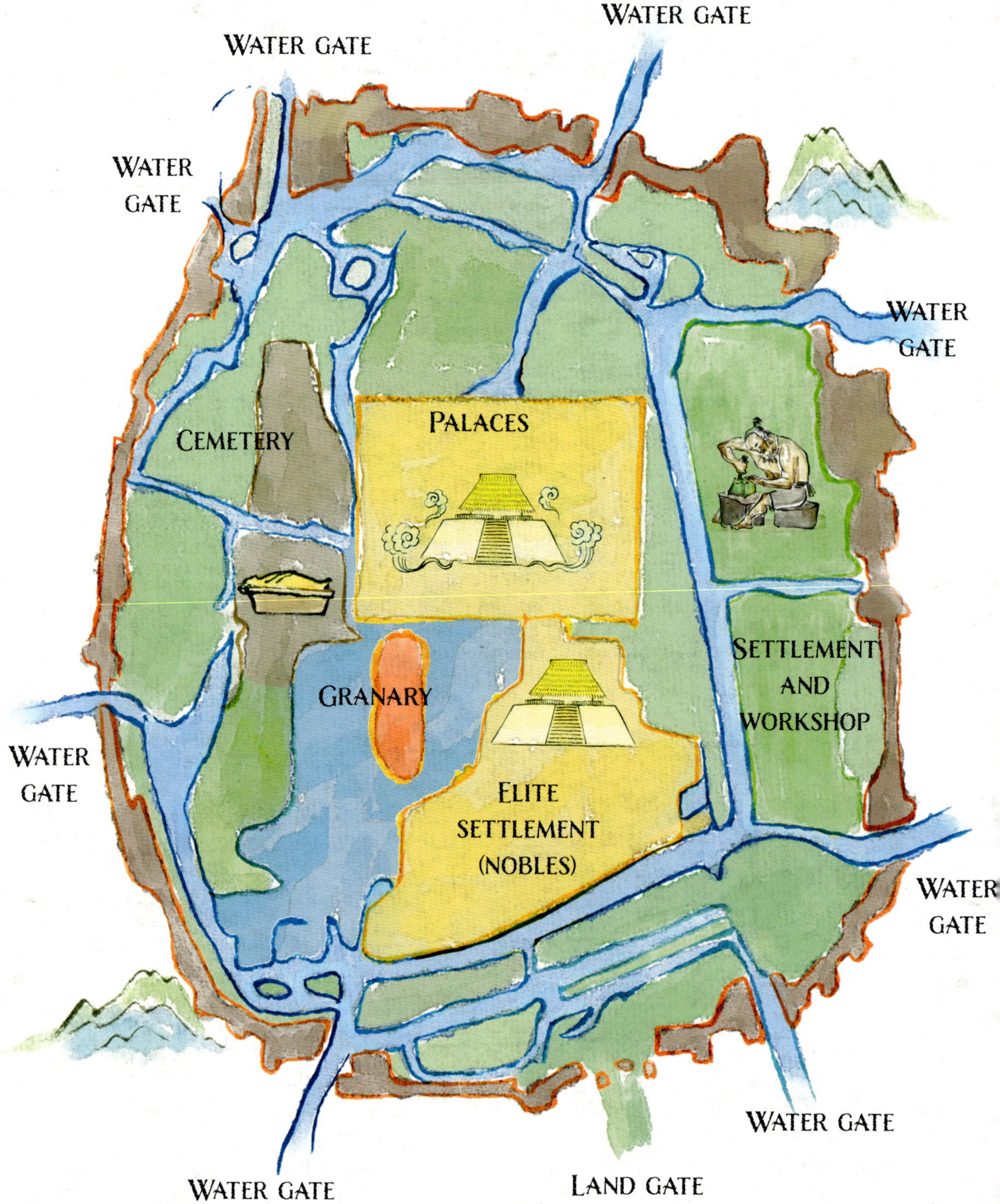
WATER GATE
WATER GATE
WATER
GATE
WATER
GATE
PALACES
CEMETERY
SETTLEMENT
AND
WORKSHOP
GRANARY
WATER
GATE
ELITE
SETTLEMENT
(NOBLES)
WATER
GATE
WATER GATE
WATER GATE
LAND GATE

Five thousand years ago, about 10,000 people lived in the ancient Liangzhu city. These residents were mainly nobles and craftsmen.

Liangzhu society had a complicated division of labour for handicrafts. There were jade makers, pottery makers, stone craftsmen and special workshops for lacquer.

KING

NOBLES

CRAFTSMEN

CARPENTER 	POTTERY MAKER 	JADE MAKER

When the number of people living in the city increased, the Liangzhu people began to build their homes outside the city.

These settlements were generally located in the highlands that bordered the city. The piers and riverbanks were reinforced with wooden supports, allowing boats to be directly pulled onto the shore.

The village of Meirendi, located to the east of the Liangzhu city, had a street plan much like a local village today.

The ancient city of Liangzhu was constructed in three concentric circles from the inside out: the palace terrace (Mojiaoshan) in the centre, the inner city around it, and the outer city around that.

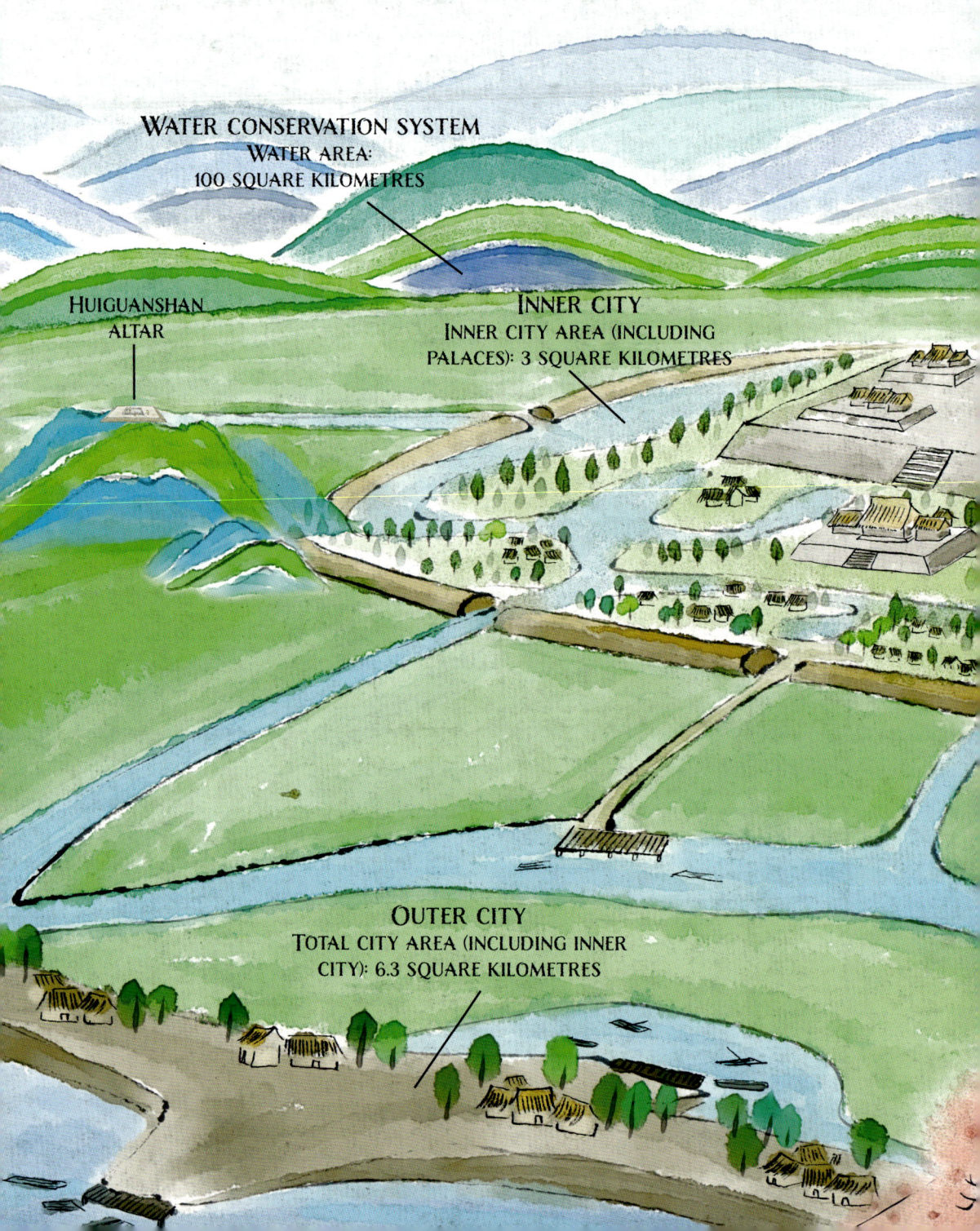

WATER CONSERVATION SYSTEM
WATER AREA: 100 SQUARE KILOMETRES

HUIGUANSHAN ALTAR

INNER CITY
INNER CITY AREA (INCLUDING PALACES): 3 SQUARE KILOMETRES

OUTER CITY
TOTAL CITY AREA (INCLUDING INNER CITY): 6.3 SQUARE KILOMETRES

This pattern is similar to the triple structure of later city settlements throughout ancient China and East Asia, which included an inner palace area, an imperial city and a larger walled city.

PALACE TERRACE (MOJIAOSHAN)
TERRACE AREA: 0.3 SQUARE KILOMETRES

YAOSHAN ALTAR

This is my dream city!

JADE

Jade is a rare, beautiful and tough mineral. The ancient Chinese first used it as an ornament more than 8000 years ago.

In the Liangzhu kingdom, jade was very popular for ornaments, and as a ritual object to show power and status - and to please the gods.

A variety of jade objects designed by the Liangzhu people have been found. Some especially fine pieces have an elaborate design carved onto them, which may have illustrated the people's religious beliefs.

The way that the ancient Liangzhu people respected and treasured jade has continued in China. In the eyes of the Chinese, a person of good character has the noble qualities of jade.

The Mountain of Floating Jade

Ancient human societies are usually divided into the 'Stone Age', 'Bronze Age' and 'Iron Age'. These names refer to the material culture of each age.

However, ancient China is a little different. In the middle to late Neolithic era – part of the Stone Age – the use of jade was common.

The Lost Book of Yue records a dialogue that happened more than 2000 years ago, which lists the tools and weapons of the ancient Chinese, in order, as stone, jade, bronze and iron.

Accordingly, some scholars have suggested that between the Stone Age and the Bronze Age, China had its own 'Jade Age'.

The Liangzhu kingdom created an impressive jade culture. In the 2000-year-old text *Shan Hai Jing (Classic of Mountains and Seas)*, Tianmu Mountain – part of the mountain range surrounding Liangzhu city – is given the beautiful name of 'The Mountain of Floating Jade'.

Jade *cong*

The *cong* tube, the *bi* disc and the *yue* axe head are the three most important ritual jades of the Liangzhu kingdom.

The *cong* is the most famous type of jade invented by the Liangzhu people. These were crafted in different shapes: some are cylindrical and some are square. Over time, the *cong* form developed from circular to square, and from shorter to taller pieces. However, all *cong* forms have a round hole through the middle, and are engraved with a unified motif on all four sides.

The largest jade *cong* that has been found so far weighs 6.5 kilograms and is 8.9 centimetres high. It is known as 'The King of *Cong*'!

In the middle part of its four-sided outer surface, eight complex sacred human and animal images were carved.

Each line carved into the jade is as narrow as a single hair, with four or five straight parallel lines within a width of 1 millimetre. Each individual line measures only 0.1 to 0.2 millimetres.

What a micro-carving master! And this was 5000 years ago! Those lines are so fine – what on earth did they use to carve them?

Did the Liangzhu people carve their jade using a metal tool?
There is currently no evidence that they used bronze or any other metals.

Some scholars suggest that the Liangzhu jades were engraved using a tool made from a very hard stone such as flint.

Did they use shark teeth or crocodile teeth?
 The indigenous people of the Amazon River in South America used piranha teeth to make saws and other tools.

Liangzhu jade definitely wasn't carved by aliens! Stay tuned to find out how the Liangzhu people did it ...

77

Jade *bi*

The *bi* disc, with a hole in the middle, was another important type of jade from the Liangzhu kingdom. Due to its circular shape, which might represent the sky or heaven, the *bi* disc was described by historians from the Bronze Age as an offering to heaven.

The *bi* discs found from the Liangzhu period were mostly plain, with no engraving. Only a few have small engraved symbols. The most common theme is a bird standing on a platform, in a pattern with four parts: a standing bird, a high column, a stepped platform, and a symbol or symbols on the platform. Some archaeologists believe that these depict scenes of sacrifice in the Liangzhu kingdom.

In the eyes of the Liangzhu people, birds were not just birds – they could also carry messages between people and their gods; between people and the sun and the moon; and between people all around the world.

The older Hongshan culture, located in the northern part of China, was also famous for its jade traditions and objects. It also used bird images but these were mainly birds of prey, such as eagles. The jade birds of Liangzhu were gentle birds, like swallows.

Because birds can fly, many human cultures have found them inspiring, and many cultures have their own myths and beliefs about birds. For example, ancient Egypt and ancient Japan had their own bird gods.

EAGLE-LIKE BIRD OF THE HONGSHAN CULTURE

SWALLOW-LIKE BIRD OF THE LIANGZHU CULTURE

SACRED IBIS OF ANCIENT EGYPT

THREE-LEGGED BIRD OF ANCIENT JAPAN

Jade *yue*

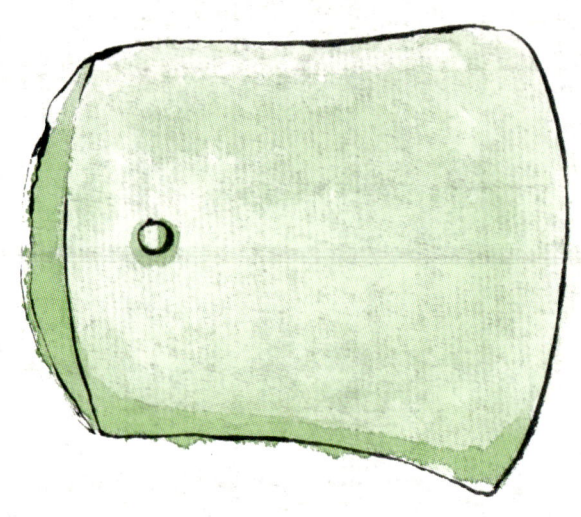

The *yue* axe jades of the Liangzhu kingdom are rarely found, so their value is particularly high.

The *yue* was a weapon like an axe, but the jade *yue* was not a weapon: it was part of a sceptre that represented power.

A jade *yue* axe includes the jade axe head, the handle, and jade ornaments for the upper end (*mao*) and lower end (*dui*) of the handle.

On one Liangzhu *yue*, known as 'The King of *Yue*', both sides are engraved with a sacred human/animal motif and a bird pattern. The engraving pattern is exquisite.

MAO – UPPER END ORNAMENT

YUE AXE HEAD

DUI – LOWER END ORNAMENT

Jade making

How were these Liangzhu jade objects made?

There were many jade workshops in the Liangzhu city. There was also a large jade workshop in what is now Deqing, in Zhejiang province, only 18 kilometres from the Liangzhu city.

There are several stages in the production of jade. These include quarrying, rough shaping and fine processing.

Step 1: Quarrying

Where does jade come from? The jade in the Liangzhu culture came from mineral resources in the mounatins.

According to the later records of the Ming Dynasty (500-600 years ago), the Liangzhu people may have obtained jade from streams, using a sieve to catch small, pebble-like pieces.

STEP 2: ROUGH SHAPING

When cutting jade, the Liangzhu craftsmen mainly used blade cutting, string cutting and tubular drilling.

Remember that this was 5000 years ago, when metal tools were not yet available. But the jade makers had a secret weapon: a particular kind of abrasive sand (*jieyusha*).

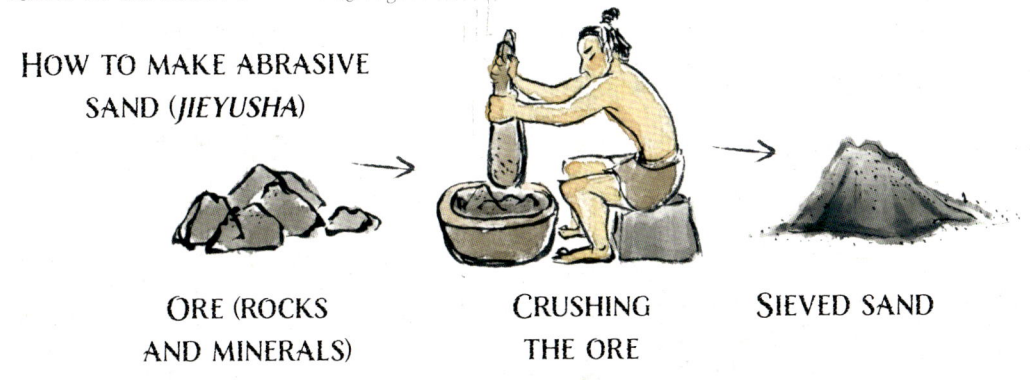

HOW TO MAKE ABRASIVE SAND (*JIEYUSHA*)

ORE (ROCKS AND MINERALS) → CRUSHING THE ORE → SIEVED SAND

BLADE CUTTING used stones or bamboo tools as thin as blades, with added abrasive sand, to roughly cut and shape the raw jade.

ABRASIVE SAND (*JIEYUSHA*)

83

STRING CUTTING was the process of cutting jade with soft string tools, adding water and abrasive sand during the process. Because the string was soft, it often left a curved cut on the surface of the jade.

The tools marks formed by these two cutting methods are completely different.

Blade cutting = straight cut
String cutting = curved cuts

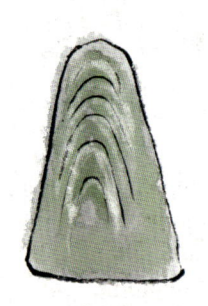

BLADE CUTTING   **STRING CUTTING**

Many jade objects from the Liangzhu period have holes in them. How did the craftsmen make these holes?

They used tube-shaped tools, along with water and abrasive sand, to drill holes in the jade.

What if the jade piece was taller than the tube-shaped tool used as a drill?

The Liangzhu people simply turned the jade object over and drilled into it from the other side.

But this led to problems if the two holes did not align properly.

Slowly, however, drilling technology improved and allowed craftsmen to drill from one side only, no matter how tall the piece of jade.

Step 3: Fine Processing

Some archaeologists suggest that there were two types of jade workers in Liangzhu: general jade makers, who found and rough-shaped the jade, and a few people - regarded as highly as wizards or priests - who were skilled enough to carve the patterns. The engraving was done using a hard, flint-type tool.

How to make a jade object

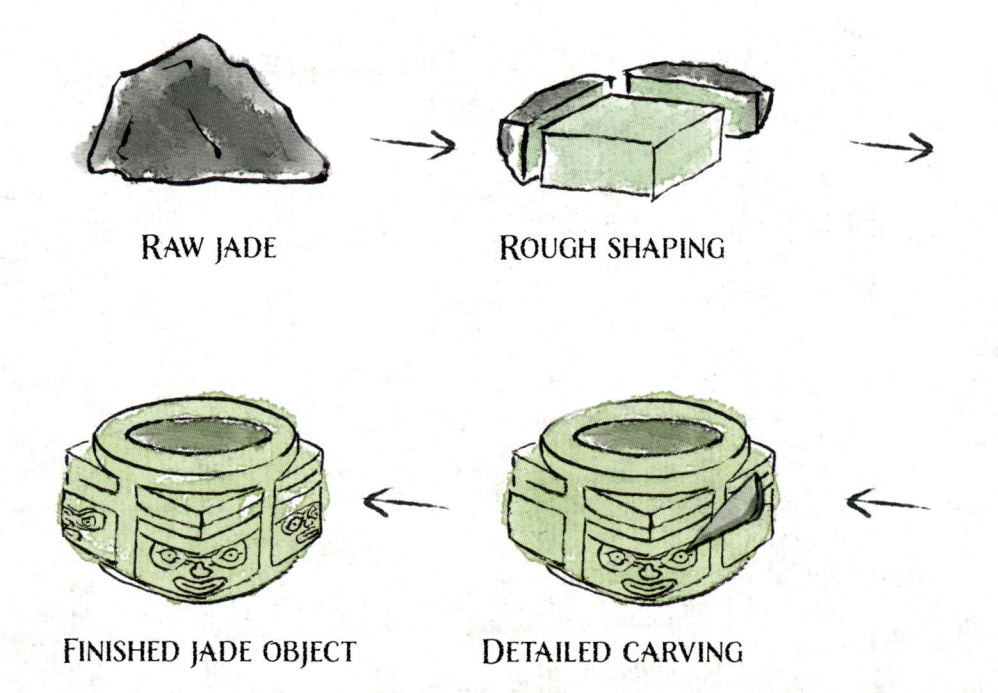

Raw jade → Rough shaping →

Finished jade object ← Detailed carving ←

SKETCHING THE SHAPES   DRILLING   POLISHING

CARVING THE PATTERN   CUTTING AND
                         SHAPING THE DETAILS

87

Using jade

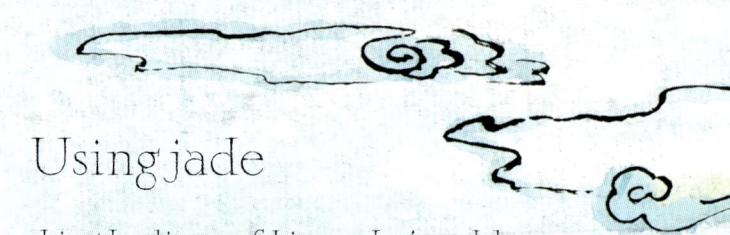

Jade was widely used in the lives of Liangzhu's nobles. They used jades for ceremonies, as ornaments, to decorate other tools, and even to make mosaics on lacquer objects.

This lacquer vase is magnificent! Look at those inlaid jades!

My lady, *please* put these jades on.
The ceremony is about to begin!

Ooh, look at this piece!
I just got it yesterday.

89

Get up early, prepare
for the ceremony...

...put on earrings,
wear my jade comb...

The Queen's Top
Jade Tips for Women

'We Liangzhu nobles can't just use any jade we like! The jade cong, bracelet, string necklace and comb can be used by men and women. But only women can use the huang pendant, the circular plaque, and the jade spindle whorl.'

BRACELET WITH DRAGON HEAD
There are four animal heads carved around this bracelet. The dragon was another god of the Liangzhu people.

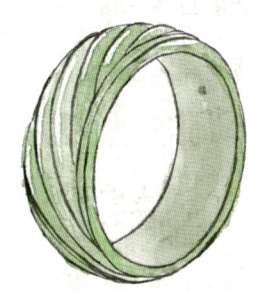

BRACELET WITH TWISTED PATTERN
So far, this is the only example of this kind of bracelet found from the Liangzhu period.

...put on bracelets and armbands...

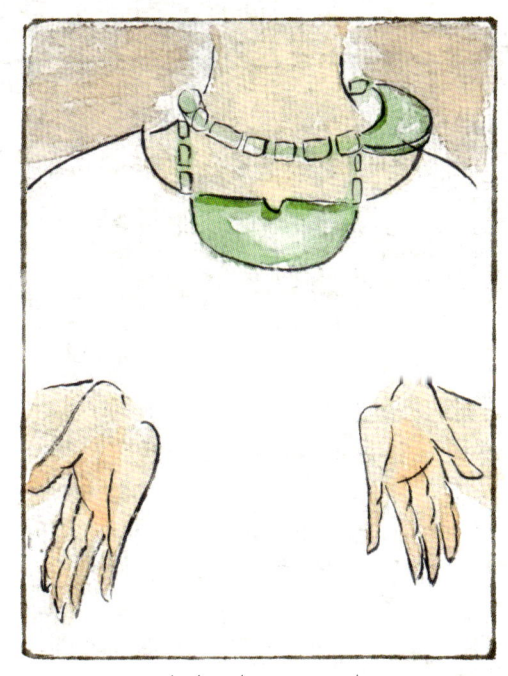

...and the *huang* pendant set, of course.

Earring

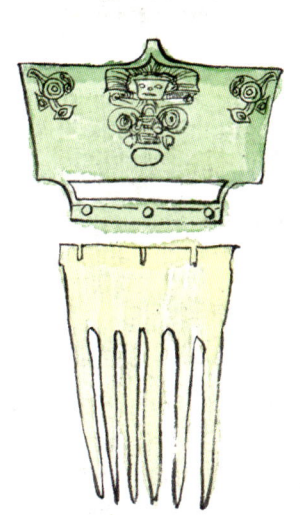

**Jade Comb Head
with Ivory Comb**

My lord, please, it's time for the sacrifice. Wakey, wakey!

Put the comb, the three-pronged headpiece and the pointed objects on the head …

The Queen's Top Jade Tips for Men

'There are certain types of jades that are only for men in our royal family.
The jade *yue* axe, the three-pronged headpiece and the pointed awl-shaped objects are for men.'

SEMI-CIRCULAR PLAQUE FOR DECORATING THE CROWN

HEADBAND FOR THE FEATHERED CROWN

THREE-PRONGED HEADPIECE

92

...put on the string necklace and bracelet...

...and don't forget the feathered crown.

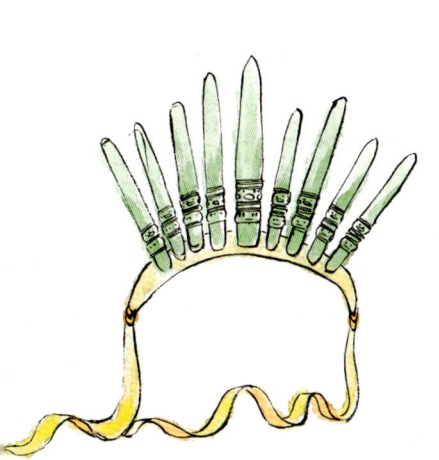

SET OF AWL-SHAPED OBJECTS FOR THE FEATHERED CROWN

Off we go!

93

The ceremony begins...

The sacrifice ceremony was the great event of the Liangzhu kingdom.

Jades were the ritual objects of the Liangzhu people, so it seems likely that they would have played a leading role in this ceremony.

Mythical motifs

The most distinctive carved motif found on jades from the Liangzhu kingdom is this sacred human/animal creature or god. It had some human qualities, but it wasn't entirely human...

It might be a human riding on an animal.

Maybe it's a half-human, half-animal god.

It could even be a sacred human playing a set of magical drums!

What is this mythical creature of Liangzhu?

What do you think?

In Chinese traditional legends, there are many half-human, half-animal gods, like the *fuxi* (a human body and a dragon's tail) and the *nvwa* (a human body and a snake's tail). The ancient Egyptians and Greeks had sphinxes with human heads and lions' bodies. The ancient Greeks told a story about the sphinx that guarded the city of Thebes and asked this riddle: 'What creature walks on four legs in the morning, two legs in the afternoon and three legs at night?'

The riddle was answered by a young man called Oedipus. His answer was 'humans'. The 'morning' is when we are babies who crawl on four 'legs'; the 'afternoon' is when we are adults and walk on two legs; and the 'night' is our old age, when we use a walking stick.

The most famous sphinx in the world is the Great Sphinx of Giza in Egypt. It was built about 4500 years ago.

In their jade carvings, the Liangzhu people also engraved the eye of their sacred human/animal figure onto the body of a bird.

The Liangzhu people had their own real-life heroes - their leaders, who built their city, managed the water system, prevented floods and made a peaceful life for all. These leaders of the kingdom might be called its 'guardians'.

Later, the Liangzhu people combined the image of their heroes with images of birds to create a new god. This god wore a feathered crown and rode a holy bird, and protected the whole kingdom.

After 1000 years of prosperity, the Liangzhu kingdom suddenly declined and disappeared. Why this happened is still a mystery.

However, the Liangzhu culture had a valuable and far-reaching influence on all the Chinese civilisations that came after it.

ABOUT THE AUTHORS

LIU BIN

刘斌

After graduating from the archaeology department of Jilin University, Professor Liu began work at the Zhejiang Provincial Institute of Archaeology and Cultural Relics in 1985 and is now the director of the Institute. He has participated in many field projects around the Liangzhu sites, including the excavations of Fanshan and Yaoshan; he also led the excavations of Huiguanshan at Yuhang, Nahebang at Jiaxing, and many other important Neolithic sites. In 2006-07, Professor Liu found the city wall of Liangzhu, based on a coring survey project he conducted. He now leads the national project on early civilisation models along the Lower Yangzte. His main interests and contributions are in prehistoric China and prehistoric jades, and his main publications include *Nan He Bang: Songze Culture Site Excavation Report*; *The Complete Collection of Jades Unearthed in China (Zhejiang volume)*; *A World of Gods and Wizards: Introduction to Liangzhu*; and the *Liangzhu City Archaeology Report*.

YU JINGJING

余靖静

As a former reporter for the Xinhua News Agency, Ms Yu has long been interested in the fields of culture and education. She has participated in reports of archaeological discoveries such as the Liangzhu ancient city (2007) and the large-scale water conservancy system (2016). She is currently CEO of Hangzhou Uwell Technology Co., Ltd. Her recent work is in using big-data technology to provide 'data portraits' of professional competence for scholars and journalists.

ABOUT THE ILLUSTRATOR
ZENG QIQI
曾奇琦

Associate Professor Zeng is the director of the Animation department at the Zhejiang University of Science and Technology. As an associate professor, her main work focuses on animation design, teaching and research on illustration, and comic creation. She has also been a visiting scholar at Drexel University, Philadelphia, USA.

ABOUT THE TRANSLATOR
QIN LING
秦岭

Associate Professor Qin teaches in the School of Archaeology and Museology at Peking University. Her main research interests are Neolithic archaeology, archaeobotany, archaeological theory and method, and prehistoric jade research.

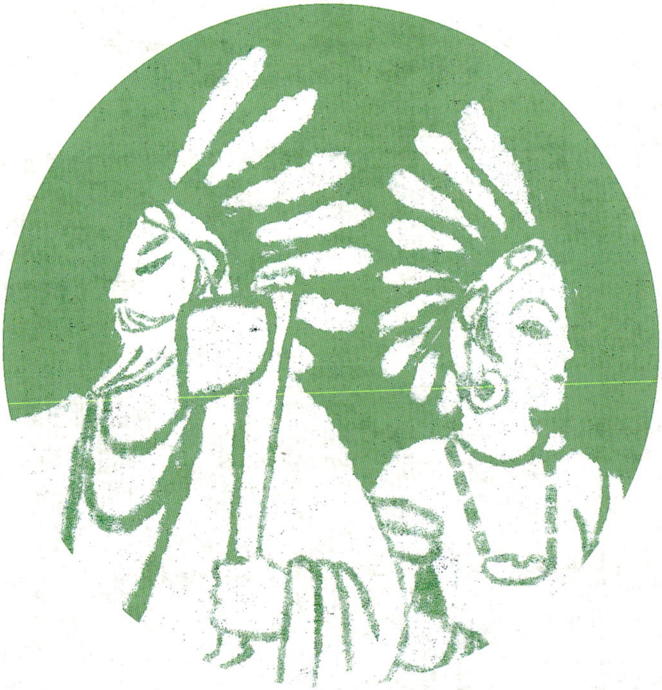